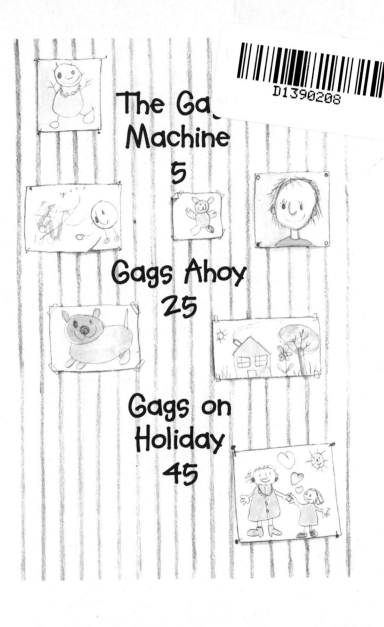

The Gags Machine

When I was very small I said "Ma Ma" and "Da Da" and "Ga Ga".

When I was bigger I said "Mummy" and "Daddy" and "Gaggy".

Now I say "Mum" and "Dad" and I call my grandma "Gags".

My dad calls Gags a machine because she works so hard.

So sometimes we call her the "Gags Machine".

7

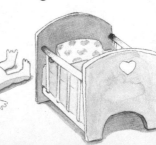

My mum is very busy with a new baby. She has to feed the baby a lot and it takes such a long time.

First the baby feeds on one side, then she feeds on the other. Next comes the burping, then the little vomits and the bib changing. Then comes the nappy changing and *the smell*. Sometimes a lot of smell!

Mum spends so much time with that baby, there's not much time left for other things.

Luckily, we have
a Gags Machine.

"Hello, Mum,"
says my mum to her
mum when Gags
comes to visit.

"How is everyone?"
says Gags as she
hurries to the laundry.

The washing
overflows the laundry
basket. It trails out
the door and down
the hallway.

"Hmph," says
Gags as she loads the washing machine.
I help her chase the socks that have
escaped into the hall.

Gags marches into the kitchen.

"Hmph," she mutters as she stares at
the piles of breakfast dishes in the sink
... and beside the sink ... and on the
stove...

I help her to stack the dishwasher.

We scrub off the crusty dried-on bits
of dog food on Leisha's bowl.

I show her where Dad exploded my
porridge in the
microwave. We

shake our heads
together.

"Hmph," we say.

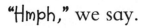

Gags pokes her head into my bedroom. It looks quite clean.

"Hmph," Gags says as she opens the wardrobe. A tennis ball rolls out and hits her on the head. There's a rumbling and a tumbling, then shoes and pyjamas and books and furry animals all topple out.

"Hmph," she says as she looks under the bed and pulls out the hidden things.

Gags points. My face feels all hot.

I quietly start to pick them up.

Next Gags gets the duster.

"Hmph," she says as she runs her finger along the window ledge. She shows me her dusty finger.

I wipe the dust off the furniture with a cloth while Gags turns into a mad vacuum-cleaning robot.

She zooms into every corner.

16

"Look out," says Gags.
Mum lifts her feet as Gags
swishes the vacuum cleaner
under them.

"Look out," says Gags again.
Mum has to lift her bottom while
Gags vacuums under the
cushions. Leisha runs away
to hide in her basket.

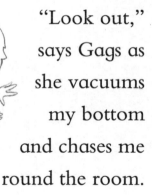

"Look out,"
says Gags as
she vacuums
my bottom
and chases me
round the room.

"Thanks, Mum," says my mum to her mum as she sits back on the couch with that baby attached.

Later, Mum goes for a lie-down. When she's not feeding the baby she makes the milk. It takes a long time and she needs lots of rest.

My mum says she's just a *milk machine*. Luckily, we have the Gags Machine.

When the baby and Mum are
sleeping, Gags and I play dress-ups.
Gags looks funny when she puts on
a floppy hat, a long dress, Dad's old
jacket and a pink feather boa. We
dance around the lounge room.

When Mum wakes up, Gags makes
tea. I lie with the baby on a mat while
Mum and Gags have a cup of tea.

I put my finger in the baby's hand
and she holds on.

She smiles at me. She smells warm
and milky and clean.

Gags puts dinner
in the oven, then
we make little
chocolate cakes.
I help her measure
the flour and sugar and
cocoa. The best part is licking
the spoon and the bowl
afterwards. Chocolate
gets all over my face
and I give Gags a
chocolatey kiss.

Then Gags waves
goodbye till next
time we get in
a pickle.

When Dad comes home, he sniffs
the air. Our house smells of cleaning
and cooking. He smiles and says, "I bet
the Gags Machine has been here."

Some machines are useful. Some
machines are fun. But nothing beats
the Gags Machine.

Gags Ahoy

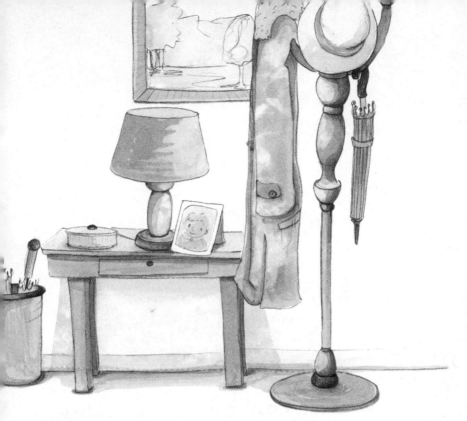

Some people call their grandma "Granny". Some people call their grandma "Gran". Some people say "Grandma" or "Nanna" or "Nan". I call my grandma "Gags".

We have a new baby. She's growing very fast. Every day she can do new things. Now she can sit up and throw things out of the pram. She can shake her rattle and laugh at my jokes. But she can't do the things that Gags can do.

Gags and I often go for walks to the park. Mum comes too. She pushes the pram and holds onto Leisha's lead.

I run ahead, but I always stop at the corner and wait for the slowcoaches to catch up.

At the park our new baby can't swing or slide or run. Mum has to sit on the bench and look after her.

But I can swing, really high. Mum worries that one day I'll swing right over the top.

I can slide so fast, I zoom
to the bottom.

And I can run
around and
around while Leisha
tries to catch me.
Gags can too but
shc's not as
good as me.

31

I climb up on top of the play equipment. Gags climbs up too but she is a bit slow.

By the time she gets to the top, she is puffing. "Not bad for an old thing," she says as she catches her breath. "Bet your mum couldn't get up here!"

"I heard that!" shouts Mum from below. She holds up the baby and points to where we are.

We play Billy Goats Gruff.
Gags is the troll and I am the
billy goats.

Gags has a big deep voice.

"Who's that trip-trapping
over my bridge?" she calls out.
She sounds just like a troll
as she hides under the
wobbly bridge.

"It's me, the littlest
billy goat," I call
out.

Gags never gets to
eat me because I turn
into the biggest billy goat
and chase her away.

Next we play princesses.
I am a princess locked
in a tower. Gags is an
evil witch, but I am very
clever and always escape.
"Ha, ha," I say as I lock
Gags in her own
tower and throw
away the key.

Then I am an evil
witch and Gags is
a princess.

36

When she escapes
I chase her around the
park on my broomstick. "I'll get
you with my zapper spell," I shout.

"Arrgh, no, please, please not the
zapper spell," cries Gags. Sometimes
I let her go. Sometimes I turn her
into a slimy toad or a slippery worm.
She can only turn back if a baby
        kisses her ... or
        a dog (*eeww*).

Next we are pirates.
I am the pirate captain and
Gags is my crew.
"Walk the plank," I say
to Gags.
Gags walks to
the end of the
equipment.
She looks down.
"Oh, please no.
There are crocodiles
and sharks and
giant squid waiting
to eat me."
"Jump!"
I command.

It's not very far but Gags
makes terrible noises
as those crocodiles
eat her.

Luckily, she comes
back to life again.

"This pirate needs a rest," Gags says, and she flops on the grass.

"Where did you hide my treasure, you naughty pirate?" I ask.

"It's in the pram," says Gags, pointing to the baby.

"She's not treasure!" I say.

Gags won't tell me where she has hidden my treasure so I make an elephant sit on her

until she does.

Gags rolls about
crying, "Help,
help, I can't
breathe … arrgh!"
Her legs kick up in the air and
then she lies still.

A man walking his dog
rushes over to Gags and starts
pulling at her coat.

"Quick, ring an ambulance,"
he shouts to Mum and
throws her his phone.

41

Gags sits up quickly. "I'm terribly
sorry, but I'm quite all right. I was just
being sat on by an elephant."

"Yes, she was a very bad pirate and
had to be punished," I say.

The man looks quite embarrassed.
I'm worried that he might be cross,
but he starts to laugh. Then Gags
starts to laugh and so does Mum.
Even the baby starts to laugh.

Gags looks down at the baby. "You'd
better hurry up and grow, little one.
I'm getting too old for this."

I hope our baby grows up soon.
I need more pirate crew.

Gags on Holiday

Our baby is getting bigger. We call her "baby" or "bubbikins" or sometimes "smellypants", but her real name is Kiera.

Kiera has kept us very busy. We've stayed home a lot. Sometimes I get bored and I think Mum does too.

But then Dad has an idea.

"It's time for a break," he says. "I've booked a caravan at the beach for the weekend."

I think that is a good idea. I need
a holiday.

"But what about the baby?" asks
Mum. Mum looks at Dad and Dad
looks at Mum.

"I can help," I say. Mum looks at
me and I look at Mum. "I can change
nappies," I say. I've watched Mum.
I know what to do.

Mum sighs. "There's so much to pack
– clothes, nappies and wipes, cot and
blanket, sunscreen and medicine. It's
a lot of work for one weekend, all that
packing and unpacking."

"Not if we also pack the Gags
Machine," says Dad.

"Yippee!" I say.

Our car's roof is piled high. Babies need a lot of things. Dad has to bang the back door closed three times.

I sit in the car. Dad fills up all the spaces around me with pillows and toys and the picnic rug.

Then Gags and the baby squish in on either side. Leisha lies on the floor at our feet.

"Look, I've used every space!" Dad says proudly to Mum.

Luckily, I can still breathe.

Leisha is a bit smelly so we have to open the windows.

"Phew," we all say.

Leisha doesn't like the car.

"It's OK, Leisha," I say. "It will be lots of fun when we get there."

51

When we get to the caravan,
Mum and Dad get out of the car,
Gags gets out of the car, and I get
out of the car, but Kiera is still asleep.
Leisha runs around in circles and barks
at the seagulls.

"Shh," we all say.

"Ah, smell that fresh sea air," says Dad.

"It smells like fun," I say.

Kiera wakes up.

"Oh, no," says Mum.

"I can help," I say. "I'll change her nappy."

"Come on then," says Gags. "Show me what you can do."

I sniff Kiera, just in case. "I don't want any nasty surprises," I tell Kiera.

I put Kiera on a mat on the bed. I undo the old nappy, clean her and then I put on a new nappy. I even put on clean pants.

"Well done," says Gags.
Kiera blows
bubbles at me.
"You're not a
smelly pants
today," I say.

Kiera has her lunch.

"Ew, what's that?" I ask Mum.

"Broccoli and carrots and pumpkin," she says.

I don't think *I* would like that if *I* was a baby. Kiera doesn't either and she spits it out all over Mum. I get Mum a cloth to wipe the browny-green goo off the end of her nose.

"Let's go to the beach," says Gags. Leisha and I run down the sandy path. Gags carries Kiera, I carry the rug and a ball, and Leisha carries the bucket in her mouth. Mum and Dad stay behind to unpack.

We find a nice flat
spot on the beach to place our rug.
I wriggle my toes in the sand. It's hot
on top, but lovely and cool below. The
tide is out so there are lots of seabirds
looking for little creatures to eat in the

shallow water. I can smell
the seaweed drying as it
crackles in the sun.

58

"We can't let you get sunburnt,"
I say as I put Kiera's hat on her head.

She pulls it off.

I put it on.

She pulls it off.

I put it on.

Gags makes a
funny face and
Kiera forgets
about the hat.

Then we let her
crawl around. Leisha lies next to her.
She likes to look after Kiera.
Kiera won't eat broccoli
and carrots but she *will* eat
sand and dirt.

Next Gags and I throw a ball.
Leisha likes this game too. I throw the
ball very high. Gags runs fast and then
she jumps. Up and up she goes.

Up and up goes Leisha.

"I've got it. I've got it," cries Gags.

"Woof, roof," barks Leisha.

Down and down Gags comes. She
doesn't see Leisha. Over goes Gags.
"Oof," says Gags.

Leisha doesn't seem to feel a thing.
Leisha is pretty tough.

Gags is a granny. She isn't so tough.
I run to get Mum and Dad.

Gags sits on a chair with her ankle on the table. We put some ice on it.

"I'm sorry, I won't be much help now," Gags says sadly.

Luckily, I am a good helper.

I play with Kiera on the bed.

"Ladies, gentlemen, babies and dogs, take your place for the great puppet show," I cry.

Mum makes Gags a cup of tea and then sits down to watch the show. Even Gags Machines need a rest sometimes.

"Starring ... Kiera the baby as ... herself."

In my show, Kiera the baby is kidnapped by the giant evil teddy bear monster. He is going to eat her. But Super Gags and I come to the rescue.

Evil teddy has to learn not to eat babies.

Babies are nice, once you get to know them. The End.

"What a great show," says Gags.

At the end of the weekend, Gags waves goodbye and says, "I think I might have a little holiday on my own now. You don't need the Gags Machine any more."

"Nonsense," says Mum. "We will *always* need our Gags Machine."

"Ga, ga," says Kiera. She thinks so too.